Once upon a SpongeBob

by James Gelsey

Illustrated by Heather Martinez

SCHOLASTIC INC.

New York   Toronto   London   Auckland   Sydney
Mexico City   New Delhi   Hong Kong   Buenos Aires

Published by Scholastic Inc.,
90 Old Sherman Turnpike, Danbury, Connecticut 06816.

SCHOLASTIC and associated logos are trademarks
and/or registered trademarks of Scholastic Inc.

ISBN 0-439-56295-3

First Scholastic Printing, April 2004

Chapters

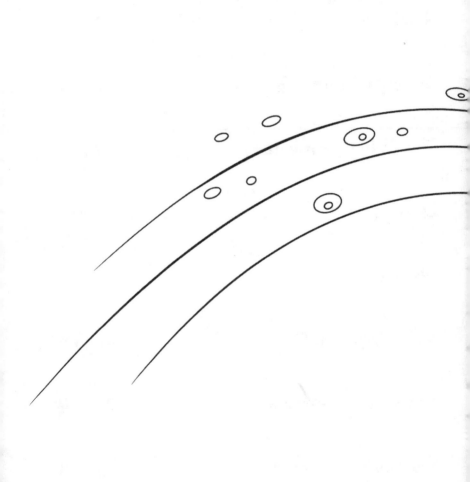

Chapter 1
Read Any Good Books Lately?

SpongeBob SquarePants was walking to work one day when something hit him on the head.

"Hey! What's the big idea?" SpongeBob cried, looking around.

"What have we here?" SpongeBob said.
He picked up a book from the ground and
read the title. "*Mother Grouper's Fairy Tales.*
Ooh, I used to love these stories when
I was little."

SpongeBob began to read. He kept reading all the way to work at the Krusty Krab.

SpongeBob read the entire day at work.

He didn't stop reading when he got home. "Wow, Gary, these fairy tales are even better than I remembered!" SpongeBob exclaimed through a mouthful of snail food.

Finally, it was time for bed.

"Gee, Gary, wouldn't it be great to live in a real fairy-tale world?" SpongeBob dreamily asked his pet. "But I know it could never happen—not in a million years . . ."

The next morning, SpongeBob awoke to the sound of Mrs. Puff calling him.

"SpongeBob!" she shouted. "Come here this instant!"

SpongeBob stumbled into the kitchen.
"Mrs. Puff!" he cried. "What are you
doing here?"

"You mean you don't recognize
your own mother?" Mrs. Puff
said in surprise. "Poor boy. I
guess not eating for two days
has affected your memory."

"SpongeBob, I want you to trade Gary for some food for us," Mrs. Puff continued.

"Trade Gary?" SpongeBob exclaimed. "Never! I wouldn't trade Gary for all the magic kelp in the sea!"

SpongeBob ran out of the house carrying Gary under his arm.

"Psst! Over here!" whispered a familiar voice. SpongeBob stared as Squidward Tentacles held out a mysterious glowing bag.

"What's that?" asked SpongeBob, entranced.

"All the magic kelp in the sea,"
Squidward answered. "How about a trade
for that snail of yours? I'll even throw in
this special bag."

"Sold!" SpongeBob said.

Mrs. Puff was furious when SpongeBob told her what had happened. She tossed the bag out the window. As soon as the bag hit the ground, a giant kelp stalk sprouted and grew higher than SpongeBob could see.

"What could be up there?" SpongeBob wondered.

SpongeBob climbed the kelp stalk to the very top. He saw a huge castle in the distance. "I can't wait to see what's inside," SpongeBob shouted, as he ran toward the castle.

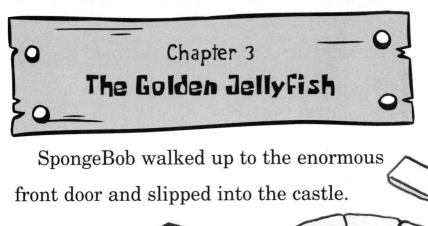

Chapter 3
The Golden Jellyfish

SpongeBob walked up to the enormous front door and slipped into the castle.

NO PEDDLERS, MEDDLERS, FIDDLERS, GRIDDLERS, TODDLERS, CODDLERS, AND ESPECIALLY NO SPONGES!

Inside, Patrick Star sat in a chair happily eating jellyfish jelly. Next to him was a beautiful jellyfish.

"Is that the jellyfish that makes the golden jelly?" asked SpongeBob in disbelief.

"It sure is," Patrick answered.

"I haven't eaten in almost three days. I'll bet that stuff tastes good," SpongeBob hinted.

"It's delicious," Patrick said, ignoring SpongeBob's hunger.

"Do you think anyone would mind if I borrowed that jellyfish for a little while?" SpongeBob hinted again.

"Naaah," Patrick said. "Well, maybe the giant."

"Giant?! What giant?" asked SpongeBob.

Suddenly the door slammed open.

"That one," Patrick
said pointing.

"Fee, fi, fo, funge, I smell the breath of a square-pantsed sponge!" shouted the giant. His thunderous steps shook the room.

"AAAAAAH!" cried SpongeBob. "Save me!"

Chapter 4
Spongerella

"AAAAAAH!" cried SpongeBob as he awoke. "Save me!" SpongeBob looked around and saw that he was in his bed.

"Wow, Gary, what a dream!" he said.

"SpongeBob!" shouted Squidward, barging into the room. "What are you still doing in bed? Sandy's fancy party is in two hours, and you've got a list of chores as long as my tentacles!"

"Sandy's having a party?" SpongeBob cheered, jumping out of bed. "Let's go!"

"You're not going anywhere until you finish your chores," Squidward said.

"What kind of chores?" asked SpongeBob.

Squidward put SpongeBob to work
helping him get ready for the party.

"I can't wait to go to Sandy's party," SpongeBob said when he finished.

"*You?* You can't go to Sandy's fancy party," Squidward said. "You don't have a fancy bone in your body. In fact, you don't have any bones in your body."

"Have a nice night, SpongeBob UnfancyPants," Squidward mocked. And he left SpongeBob all alone.

"Gee, Gary, I really wish I could go to Sandy's party," SpongeBob said sadly.

Suddenly there was a flash of light and a strange-looking character appeared.

"Never fear!" came a deep, gravelly voice. "Your Fairy Krabmother is here!"

Chapter 5
Abrakakrabra!

The Fairy Krabmother led SpongeBob outside.

"Now let's make this the fanciest night of your life!" the Fairy Krabmother said.

The Fairy Krabmother turned a Krabby Patty into a coach and hitched a team of jellyfish to the front to pull it.

Patrick saw the magic and quickly ran over.

"Turn me into something!" he begged.

"C'mon, please!"

The Fairy Krabmother waved
her magic wand and *Poof!*

"Whee! I'm
an umbrella!"
Patrick sang.

"Now let's do something
about those rags," the
Fairy Krabmother said
to SpongeBob.

"Now remember, the magic wears off at midnight, me boy," the Fairy Krabmother warned.

"Thanks, Fairy Krabmother!" SpongeBob said. He jumped into the coach and sped off to the party.

Chapter 6
A Kickin' Good Time

SpongeBob arrived at the Treedome for Sandy Cheeks's fancy party. He immediately caught Sandy's attention.

"You're lookin' pretty fancy," she told SpongeBob. "How about a turn around the dance floor?"

Sandy pulled him onto the dance floor. Together, they karate-danced all night.

"Say, you're the best karate dancer I've ever seen!" Sandy gushed. "What's your name?"

Before SpongeBob could answer, the clock began striking midnight.

"Sorry, gotta go!" he yelped. He raced from the Treedome but dropped something along the way.

Sandy looked down.

"I must find the stranger who fits in
these pants!" she declared.

Sandy searched all of Bikini Bottom but couldn't find the pants' rightful owner. Finally, she ended up at SpongeBob's house.

Sandy called SpongeBob outside. He quickly put on the square pants.

"A perfect fit! You're the one!" Sandy exclaimed, as she karate-danced toward him. "Haiiiiii-YAH!"

"Haiiiiii-YAH!" SpongeBob awoke
with a start.

"Wow, Gary, what a dream within a dream!" he said.

"Meow!" Gary said.

"What do you mean I look different?" SpongeBob asked.

SpongeBob looked at himself in the mirror. "Aaaaaah!" he shrieked. "I'm not SpongeBob anymore. I'm—I'm—KrabbyPattyBob! And this isn't my bed! It's a griddle!"

SpongeBob jumped off the griddle, but Mr. Krabs blocked the way.

"And where do you think you're going, me little Krabby Patty?" asked Mr. Krabs.

KrabbyPattyBob ducked between Mr. Krabs's legs and took off.

"Come back here!" Mr. Krabs yelled, chasing after him.

"Run, run, run as fast as you can," KrabbyPattyBob called back. "You can't catch me, I'm the Krabby Patty Man!"

Outside, KrabbyPattyBob was quickly surrounded by a hungry mob.

"What's cooking, everybody?" he asked nervously.

"You are, KrabbyPattyBob!" Sandy answered.

"But you wouldn't eat me like this . . .

would you?" stammered KrabbyPattyBob.

"Naw, of course not," reassured Sandy.

"First we'd have to get some fries and a drink!"

"Hellllp!" cried KrabbyPattyBob.

53

Chapter 8

Happily Ever After

Just then Patrick jumped out to protect KrabbyPattyBob from the threatening crowd.

"Stop!" Patrick shouted. "Has not a Krabby Patty feelings? If you prick him with a fork, will not his delicious juices escape and make your fries all soggy?"

"I hate when that happens," said someone in the crowd.

"Me, too," agreed another. The crowd wandered away, leaving Patrick and KrabbyPattyBob all alone.